Grumpy Cat®

LOVE AND GRUMPINESS

By Frank Berrios

Illustrated by Steph Laberis

A Random House PICTUREBACK® Book

Random House New York

grumpycats.com
rhcbooks.com
Educators and librarians, for a variety of teaching tools, visit us at RHTeachersLibrarians.com
ISBN 978-0-593-11912-9
MANUFACTURED IN CHINA
10 9 8 7 6 5 4 3 2

Early one morning, the doorbell rang. *DING-DONG!*
   "Go away," said a sleepy Grumpy Cat.
   Thankfully, Pokey was wide awake—he was a morning kitty.
"I'll get it!" he said as he raced to the door.

"Flower delivery for Pokey and Grumpy Cat. Happy Valentine's Day!" said the delivery dog. "Thank you," replied Pokey. "I almost forgot today is Valentine's Day! It's one of my favorite holidays!"

"Valentine's Day was invented to sell cards," mumbled Grumpy Cat.

"These flowers are so beautiful," said Pokey.
"And they smell great."

Suddenly, the doorbell rang.
DING-DONG!
"Not again," grumbled
Grumpy Cat.

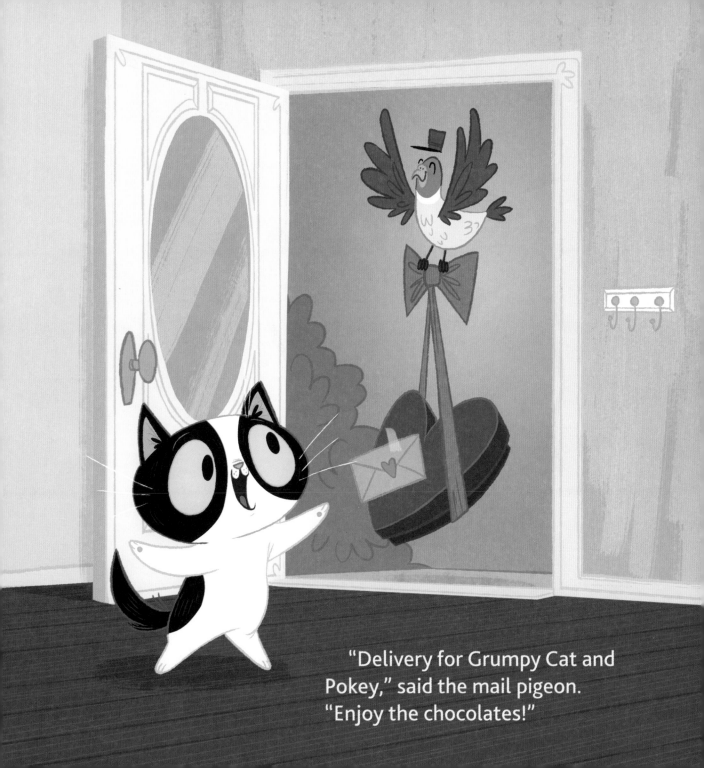

"Delivery for Grumpy Cat and Pokey," said the mail pigeon. "Enjoy the chocolates!"

"Chocolate? I like chocolate,"
admitted Grumpy Cat.
Now she was interested!

"Yes, chocolate! It's delicious!" said Pokey.
"And after we eat the candy, we can play
with the wrappers!"

**"You are so easily entertained,"
replied Grumpy Cat.**

All day long, cards arrived. Each one was special and unique—just like their friends.

"This one's from Iguana! And this one has to be from Unicorn!" said Pokey. "Yep, I was right!"

"Let's make Valentine's Day cards for our friends!"
suggested Pokey. "We have tape, crayons, paper, and glue."

"No, no, no, and no," replied Grumpy Cat.

"C'mon, it'll be fun. Let's get silly with it!"
**"I don't do 'silly,'" replied Grumpy Cat
as Pokey got started.**

"This one's for Butterfly! And this one's for Ladybug!"
squealed Pokey. He was having a great time!

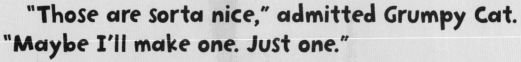

"Those are sorta nice," admitted Grumpy Cat.
"Maybe I'll make one. Just one."
    "Yay!" cheered Pokey. "Here's some glitter and glue
and . . . whoops!"

"I'm done," said Grumpy Cat.

"But Valentine's Day is all about giving," pleaded Pokey. "Our friends sent us flowers, cards, and candy today. We need to do something nice for them, too!"

Grumpy Cat agreed. "You're right.
Pass the glitter. Carefully this time."

Before long, Pokey and Grumpy Cat had made cards
for all their friends. And they finished just in time!

DING-DONG!
"It's our friends," exclaimed Pokey.
"What a wonderful surprise!"

Valentine's Day was a success. But Grumpy Cat was glad it only came around once a year. It was going to take forever to get all that glitter out of the house!